Trip

A Random House

A lot of money

Sallys car is broken

A Scary Doll

My scary and fantastic trip

I was so stressed that I forgot to bring coffee with me when I was going to meet some bosses. I heard that my colleague Kathrine did get money from my boss and she did get them that day she was pregnant and my boss also gave her some trip tickets and he knew that she was pregnant and he said that if she can't, she can give the trip tickets to someone else. When I was sitting on the couch in my office Katherine came to me and said "I want to give you my trip tickets".

I was literally confused and I was also surprised I didn't think that my best friend Kathrine would give me her trip tickets. I said thank you to Kathrine many times and hugged her. She said that I was going to travel to Dubai, Turkey, and Afghanistan. She also said that I have to be in Turkey for three weeks, in Dubai I have to be there for two weeks, and in Afghanistan for three weeks.

So I was at the airport and I had my bag and my clothes and everything I needed. I saw the schedule of the flight and I saw the Turkish Airlines it stood they would travel ten past ten. I was so confused because Kathrine said that I have to go early to not come late to Turkish Airlines. It took like ten or eleven hours to arrive in Turkey. I was finally in Turkey and I was so happy to be there. I met the Turkish president Recep Tayyip Erdoğan. The president of Turkey was so nice and kind he invited me for tea and Turkish snacks. We were talking about Turkey and the cultures and the food and also the snacks. He gave me an address to a hotel and he said he would rent it. So I went to the hotel and it was so beautiful. The clock was twelve and I was in the hotel's game room and I was so tired so I went to my bedroom and slept.

Next day I saw a package outside my hotel room. And it was a paper in it and it said "Do you wanna go out and have picnic in forces". I was so confused so I took my phone and I called Kathrine. She answered me and I said to her that it's a box outside the door. She said that she sent the box to her sister to give it to me. Kathrine screamed and said that I'm going to picnic in a place called "burak" with her sister.
I was surprised and also excited so I bought a very expensive necklace for her sister. I took a extra shirt with me and some strawberries I love. I was so confused about the name "burak" so I asked Katherine's sister Sailly why the name was so. Because I know that burak means like stop or something like that.

I googled the forest called burak and it was not that far away. Sailly had a car so she drove me. We were finally at burak and it was so beautiful the view was amazing. I saw a bench and Sailly went to it and took her blanket on that and did a decoration on the bench. The bench was finally ready. I sat on the bench. I took the necklace from my bag and I gave it to Sailly and she said you didn't have to. And then she said thank you many times and she also asked me how much money I paid to the necklace I said that I only spent like 300 lira or something. She screamed and said did you spend 21 dollars on a necklace. I said to her it's fine can you can relax.

Sailly saw a suitcase with a lot of money near a big tree. We went to it and we looked at the money to see if it was real or not. Then Sailly stared at the money a lot and then I told her that we had to go. The sun was almost completely down and we went to Sailly`s car and we saw that the car was broken. Sailly was stressed and she got very angry and immediately picked up her mobile and started to see if it was possible to call someone for help. Afterwards, she asked me if I had two flashlights with me. I said that I have, she run away somewhere and I didn`t know where so I got my own flashlight and I looked everywhere and finally I found her. She was stuck in a bush.
We ran so much that we lost our energi. We were finally at a house and we got in there and we slept there.

Sailly screamed so badly that my heart was pounding so fast and hard. She said that she saw a very scary doll who had a huge number of teeth. I asked where she saw the doll and she said under the bed, so I checked under the bed and then the doll just came on my face and it scared the life out of me. Both me and Sailly got scared and we ran out of the house, the doll was looking out of the broken window and we ran away as fast as we could. I saw a bus and I told Sailly to run as fast as I did, she caught up with me and we both got into the bus and the busdriver asked if we had a bus card and we both said that it was an emergency and he said that it was okay.

Then after like one or two hours we both finally came to my hotel in Istanbul, I asked Sailly if she wanted to sleep over, and she said okay. I did get a nightmare and in the nightmare I saw the doll I saw in the creepy house I and Sailly went to and slept there. I took up my mobile and it was 2 o'clock at night or something like that, I went to the rum Sailly were slept I wanted to check if she was good asleep and I saw that she was asleep and when I was turning round for a second I saw a scary doll, the doll had magic power and when I was running to the door she close the door with her power.
The doll turned into Sailly and I was very terrified.

Sailly told me that a monster turned her into a creepy doll in the night and a normal girl during the day. We talked about how to get rid of the spell, she told me that I don't have to be afraid of her and she said that she has a sister called Maiana and she is the only one who knows how to break the spell. Sailly also told me that Maiana Lives in Afghanistan. Sailly called her sister Maiana by face timing her and I also talked to Maiana and I told her that I would visit Afghanistan. After some hours Sailly went to her own house.

The next day I wondered when I would travel to Afghanistan. So I went to the president of Turkey and I took my backpack and my trip tickets and also my passports. I was finally in his office and I met him and I asked him when I was going to travel to Afghanistan. He said that Dubai international airport was canceled and that he did talk to my boss and that I would travel to Afghanistan instead. My weeks in Turkey were soon over and I had only two days left there. I spent those two days with my cousin Narina. We went to many parks and we ate ice cream and we had a lot of fun. I had only a couple of hours in Turkey so I said goodbye to the president, Sailly, and my cousin Narina. Narina was very sad because she had not seen me in years. I was at the Turkish airlines and I saw the schedule of the flight and it said they would travel to kabul ten past twenty. I was so excited and I had a huge stomach ache on the planet when I was going to eat fish. I have not visited Afghanistan since I was like 9 years old so I had a little problem with the plan. I checked the date and that was july 19 th, 2021. It took like 14 hours to travel to Afghanistan. Yes. I was finally in Afghanistan and my stomach didn't hurt anymore.

I went to my cousin Lemay and I asked her if I could live in her house for 2 weeks or something. She said that I was welcomed and I said thankyou to her many times. She gave me a room in her house and I took my clothes and put them on the wardrobe and I took some clothes with me so I could put them on before I go to Sailly`s sister Maiana's house and ask her about some antidote. I took my mobile and my backpack with me and went to Maiana`s house and I called her on the number Sailly sent to me. I was finally at her door and she opened to me. She was so beautiful and she wore a hijab. She asked me

- Are you the girl my sister Sailly was talking about?
- Yes I am.
- Oh it's nice to meet you
- Thanks, I was about to ask you about something.
- What do you wanna ask me?
- I wanna make sure that you have the antidote with you.
- Of course I have

-   Can I come in?
-   yes

Maiana showed me her house and everything, and she said that I can be in her room so she can bring the antidote from another room. She came to her room and gave me the antidote and I thanked her and I put the antidote in my backpack`s little bag and I closed all the lightning chains in my bag. I was about to say goodbye to her but she said to me that she wanted me to stay for 10 minutes more. So I asked her some questions and she told me that she has three cousins in the city Mazar-e Sharif and they go to a school where they learn Turkish also and that their school is about to shut down. I felt so bad after hearing that so I gave Maiana 200 dollars and she was about to cry. She thanked me and I gave her a little bag I bought from Turkish Airlines as a present and I said goodbye to her. When I was going out, Maiana gave me two tickets to a concert.

A week later I put on a very beautiful dress and I called my cousin Asina and I told her about the concert in Kabul, and she was actually freaked out. Asina went to my home and I gave her a green traditional dress and she put on the dress in my room, and then we both went to the concert. We saw Aryana Sayeed in the concert and she looked amazing. I said to Asina that I have heard her before and her music. Asina told me that she doesn't really like her. When Asina told me, I was thinking about my friend Ilayda. My friend Ilayda didn't like it when I started one of Aryana's songs. Ilayda likes to listen to a girl called Nahima. I and Asina had a lot of fun and some singers gave us cake and snacks.

One day after the concert, I went to a restaurant and I chosed a meal, and I took up my mobile and I looked at the clock and then the battery was gone. I took my trip tickets and I looked when I was travel back to Sweden again, and it said, August 8, 2021. Asina was calling me by facetime and she asked me if I wanna spend one week with her. I said yes of course.
I went to her house and she told me that she have little courtyard, I was so surprised because I had missed that. I asked her if we could have picnic or something, she said she would like to have picnic in the yard.

I spend three days with Asina and we both had fun and we went to so many parks in Kabul. My friend Sahra was also an Afghan but she was from another ethnic group called the Hazaras. We both are different, she is hazaras and I am pashtun and we don't speak the same language but I can speak little dari not the whole language and our language is the same when we say something. I still understand Sahra. Sarah`s mom invited me and Asina to her house, and we went there.

 I saw Sarah's mom cooking Kabuli rice for us in the kitchen, so I went to her and said that she didn't have to do kabuli rice for us. Sarah's mom said it's not so hard to make Kabuli rice. I helped her with the salad and other things in the kitchen. In the capital of Afghanistan, you do not eat at the table you then eat on the ground in your house, So Sarah's sibling came from a supermarket in Kabul with their father called Norri, and they greeted us and we all washed our hands before a really good meal. I ate so many meals and it tasted so delicious and so good. Then after an hour we played carts and we decided to play 4 times without losing, and win up to 1500 afghani.
I and Asina stayed in Sarah`s house for four days and we went to so many bars and restaurants. Asina went to a bar and bought a new hijab for Sarah's mom that day.
Asina and I said goodbye to Sarah`s family, and then I said to Asina that I have to go home to my grandma in Meral`s house to

tell her that I only have like 5 days left in Afghanistan. Asina said that it was okay and she went to her home and I went to my grandma.

I went to my grandma and we had a lot of fun. I gave her like 4500 afghans to buy bread,butter,flour and sugar and everything else she needed. My grandma and I went to many bars and we did buy many things and we also bought culture jewelry. I checked a hotel in Kabul and I found a good one where my grandmother and I would spend three days there. I gave Asina the location of the hotel. My grandmother and I went to the hotel and we spent three days there. We invited our cousins and our friends to the hotel and we had a good time there.

A day later I said goodbye to my grandmother and I went to Meral`s house. I and Meral cooked some meals and she saw my trip tickets and said do you have like two days left in Afghanistan?"

I told her that I wanna spend only one day with her, she said it was okay. My boss called me and said that I have to go to a restaurant called "Bolanis". Next I got out of Meral`s house when it was sunrise and I started walking to the restaurant and my boss called me by facetime and we talked about my trip tickets. He told me that I`m gonna travel back to Sweden in about a few hours. My boss and I talked a lot, and then we said goodbye to each other and I went to Meral`s house and

I packed my bag and everything else that was left and when I was finally ready with everything, I took my mobile and started to see one news item on my google page, and I tapped it and it was about the Taliban. The Taliban took over some parts of Afghanistan, I was so scared so I called my colleague and she told me that the Taliban were taking over some parts and they are about to take over Kabul soon. I called my boss and told him that the Taliban would soon be here and that I would soon be on my way to Sweden, and that I needed all the help to get back to Sweden so that I would be safe. I took my bag where I had antidote and everything I had from Meral`s house and I ran for help to the Turkish Airlines.

I was so glad that I got into the Turkish
Airlines and I was about to go home to
Sweden Again. I was in Turkey and I saw
Sailly come in and run to me and hug me
and say thank you so much. I gave Sailly
the antidote and she said you are a
lifesaver. I found out that my flight was
about to fly in a few minutes so I said
goodbye to Sailly and got on the flight back
to Sweden. It took 12 hour to travel back to
Sweden and I was finally there. I went to
my job and it was dark in all the offices. My
colleague and my friends surprised me
with a big cake and we had a party in my
office.

The End